WAITING FOR THE

Great Pumpkin

WAITING FOR THE

Great Pumpkin

CHARLES M. SCHULZ

FANTAGRAPHICS BOOKS, SEATTLE

True Love Revealed in the Pumpkin Patch

10-16

SCHULZ

WAITING FOR THE GREAT PUMPKIN
Charles M. Schulz

Editor: Gary Groth
Designer: Jacob Covey
Associate Publisher: Eric Reynolds
Publisher: Gary Groth

Special thanks to Marcie Daniel for her invaluable assistance.

Fantagraphics Books, 7563 Lake City Way NE, Seattle, WA 98115, USA. For a free
full-color catalog of comics, call 1-800-657-1100. Our books may be viewed
and purchased on our website at www.fantagraphics.com.

ISBN 978-1-60699-772-7
First printing: September 2014
Printed in China

Thanks to: Randall Bethune, Big Planet Comics, Black Hook Press of Japan, Nick Capetillo, Kevin Czapiewski,
John DiBello, Juan Manuel Domínguez, Mathieu Doublet, Dan Evans III, Thomas Eykemans, Scott Fritsch-Hammes,
Coco and Eddie Gorodetsky, Karen Green, Ted Haycraft, Eduardo Takeo "Lizarkeo" Igarashi, Nevdon Jamgochian,
Andy Koopmans, Philip Nel, Vanessa Palacios, Kurt Sayenga, Anne Lise Rostgaard Schmidt, Christian Schremser,
Secret Headquarters, Paul van Dijken, Mungo van Krimpen-Hall, Jason Aaron Wong, and Thomas Zimmermann